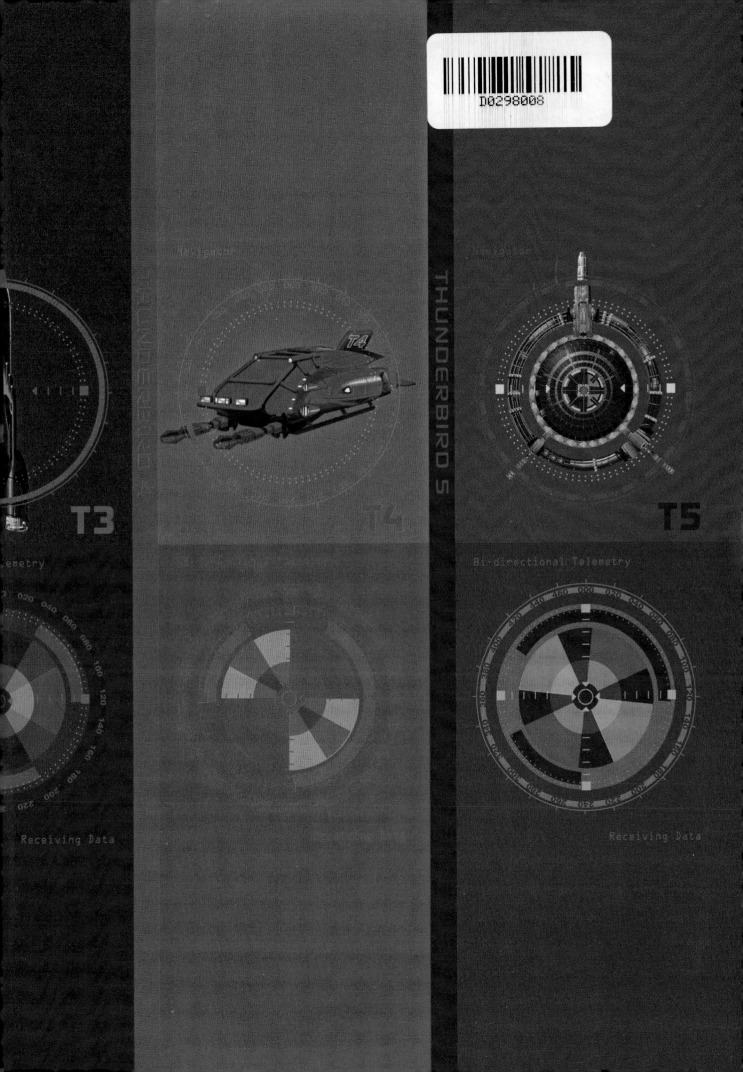

T3

T4

T5

THUNDERBIRD 3

THUNDERBIRD 4

THUNDERBIRD 5

Navigator

Navigator

...emetry

Bi-directional Telemetry

Receiving Data

Receiving Data

THIS THUNDERBIRDS ANNUAL
BELONGS TO

Jordan Bhatt (Hood) pg 17

CONTENTS

Team Tracy	8
Thunderbirds: Chapter 1	10
Allies ... and Enemies	16
IR Skills Assessment: 1	18
FAB 1	20
Thunderbirds: Chapter 2	22
IR Skills Assessment: 2	28
Thunderbirds: Chapter 3	30
Thunderbirds: the Fleet	
Thunderbird 1	36
Thunderbird 2	38
Thunderbird 3	40
Thunderbird 4	42
Thunderbird 5	44
Thunderbirds: Chapter 4	46
Thunderbirds: Rescue Vehicles	52
IR Skills Assessment: 3	54
Thunderbirds: Chapter 5	56
IR Skills Assessment: 4	62
Thunderbirds: Chapter 6	64

Written and compiled by Sarah Ripley

Based on a motion picture screenplay by William Osborne and Michael McCullers
Story by Peter Hewitt and William Osborne.

Original television series conceived by TTC Distribution, LLC
Designed by Craig Cameron and Garreth Williams

TEAM TRACY

This heroic adventure is about the members of one family who have dedicated their lives to saving the world from disaster.

In the year 2010 ex-astronaut and billionaire Jeff Tracy lost his wife in a tragic accident. He took what was left of his family, his five young sons, to a remote tropical island in the Pacific Ocean to try to rebuild their lives.

T3

JEFF ( )

T1

SCOTT ( )

T2

VIRGIL ( )

There, in his wife's memory, Jeff built not just a new home, but the headquarters of a secret organization he called International Rescue.

The team members are totally dedicated to helping those in need wherever and whenever disaster strikes. For this elite group of heroes, coming to the aid of the world is all in a day's work.

From a state-of-the-art satellite, they monitor events across the globe. At their command is the most technologically advanced fleet of craft ever known to man. The Thunderbirds are five extraordinary vehicles equipped to handle any type of disaster.

Thanks to their work, Jeff Tracy and his sons have now come to be known by the name they gave their incredible team of machines:

THUNDERBIRDS ™

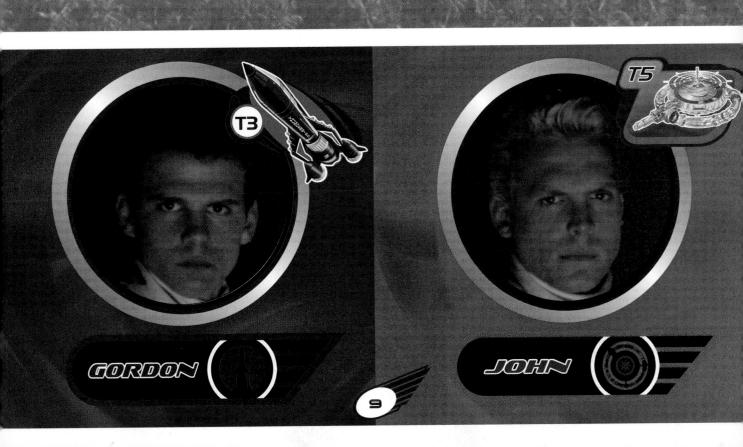

T3

T5

GORDON

JOHN

It was the last day of term at Wharton Academy, a boarding school in upstate New York, and fourteen-year-old Alan Tracy was looking forward to going back to his Pacific island home for the holiday. So was his best friend, Fermat Hackenbacker.

When another student ran past them, heading for the common room and yelling, "Turn on the TV! It's the Thunderbirds!" they took off after him.

The common room was already full. A crowd of students pushed and shoved to get the best view of the big plasma-screen TV.

Alan and Fermat pushed to the front of the crowd as Lisa Lowe reported from a helicopter hovering in front of a huge oil-drilling rig that burned above an angry sea.

"Disaster in the Bering Strait," she told a watching world. "Six workers are trapped on the burning rig. Fire damage means it's in danger of total collapse." She paused. "The only hope is the Thunderbirds."

Seeing something approaching in the sky above her, she pointed. "And here they are!"

As Alan watched, a rocket-like aircraft with swept wings zoomed into view and circled the platform. Thunderbird 1 was piloted by Alan's brother, Scott Tracy, who used its vertical take-off and landing engines to hold it steady as he assessed the scene.

As Alan and the other students watched, Thunderbird 2, piloted by his father, Jeff, swept across the screen, a massive green turtle-shaped fuselage with small front-swept wings and a huge tail fin on its back.

"It looks like the Thunderbirds are going to attempt a rescue," Lisa reported, as Thunderbird 2 swept in low over the rig. It lurched violently, very nearly colliding with the platform, as the updraft from the flames hit it.

The students gasped.

"Come on, Dad!" Alan whispered to himself. He couldn't speak out loud because everything about International Rescue was top secret. Only Fermat knew that Alan was one of the Tracy brothers, and that was because his own dad was an important part of the team …

Thunderbird 2 hovered close to the rig as the workers edged along a scaffold and away from the smoke and flames moving towards them. Then a

hatch opened and a circular escape lift was lowered down to them.

A huge wave slammed into the scaffold and the rig lurched so violently that the workers were knocked off their feet. They slid down towards the churning waters …

Just as they seemed doomed, six rescue lines shot out from the rescue platform of Thunderbird 2 and clamped themselves around the workers. Then Thunderbird 2 lurched up and wheeled away, towing them behind.

It was not a second too soon: a pylon buckled and the scaffold crashed into the sea.

The students cheered as the workers were winched into the safety of Thunderbird 2's mighty fuselage.

"Unbelievable," said Lisa Lowe. "As always, the Thunderbirds are working in total secrecy. We know nothing about them. What we do know is that those trapped men would not have survived without their efforts. When disaster strikes, the world has come to depend on them."

But the job wasn't done yet, because the fire was raging more powerfully than ever.

Now it was Scott Tracy's turn to act. He piloted Thunderbird 1 towards the rig and fired a powerful missile at the plume of flaming oil. It detonated overhead and the explosion that followed filled the air with smoke, sea water and steam. But it did just what Scott intended: robbed the fire of the oxygen that fed it and extinguished the blaze.

"The fire is out!" Lisa reported. "The Thunderbirds have done it again!"

As the students watched, the injured rig workers were ferried off to safety.

But Alan's celebrations were interrupted by the arrival of the headmaster. "Tracy," he said. "There's someone here to see you."

The visitor was Lady Penelope Creighton-Ward. Her looks always caused a stir, and today was no different.

"Alan, your father has asked me to pick you up," she said, glancing at the TV screen. "He has been … unexpectedly delayed."

●●●

Minutes later, Alan and Fermat were outside their dorm with their cases. Alan grinned at Lady Penelope. "Why are you here? Are you on a mission?"

"Ssshh!" said Lady Penelope. "I'm an undercover agent, remember?"

As she spoke, FAB 1, her long, low, sleek and purring ultra-fast six-wheeled limousine drew up alongside them. It was sprayed pink to match her clothes and was driven by her butler and chauffeur, Parker.

"Hop in, boys," said Lady Penelope.

Parker drove out of the school grounds

and accelerated down the highway. He pressed buttons on the dash and a small screen dropped from the brim of his cap. Data readouts like those in the cockpit of a fighter jet appeared on the screen, and Parker accelerated even more.

Alan and Fermat looked at each other. What was he doing? They were on a winding road that clung to a steep cliff edge. He was going way too fast to take the upcoming curve safely!

As the boys stared in horror, Parker turned the wheel sharply to the left and the car shot right off the edge of the cliff and into thin air!

They gripped the armrests as the car plunged towards the valley far below. There was a sudden power surge from FAB 1's modified jet engines and the car sprouted wings! It banked and soared up through the clouds.

Alan and Fermat looked at each other, then smiled and high-fived. They were travelling to Tracy Island in SOME style!

•••

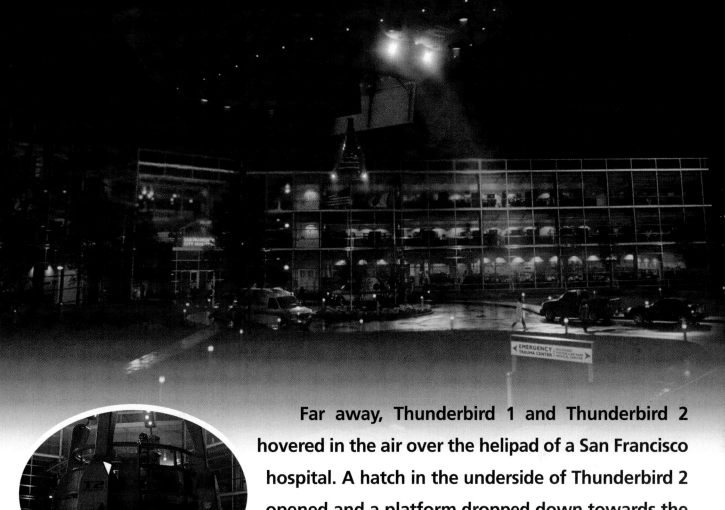

Far away, Thunderbird 1 and Thunderbird 2 hovered in the air over the helipad of a San Francisco hospital. A hatch in the underside of Thunderbird 2 opened and a platform dropped down towards the waiting hospital staff. On it were the six rescued oil rig workers …

No one noticed when one of them pressed a secret switch on his belt and a tiny projectile shot out of his buckle and arced towards Thunderbird 1. The micro-missile hit the mighty machine's nose cone and splashed a small amount of a fluorescent chemical material onto the fuselage. Unseen, the liquid quickly spread over the surface and seeped deep into the craft's metal skin …

Their mission complete, and unaware of what had happened, the Thunderbirds wasted no time and zoomed off into the night.

continued on page 22 …

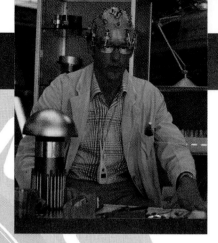

The work of International Rescue depends on Jeff Tracy, his sons – and Thunderbirds 1, 2, 3, 4 and 5. But they couldn't do what they do without the talents and skills of a great back-up team.

Professor Fermat Hackenbacker is known to everyone as Brains. That's because he's the technical genius behind International Rescue. He's the one who keeps the mighty Thunderbirds fleet at the ready, and mans the computers and command centre. He's indispensable.

Brains' son is called **Fermat**. He's still young, but it looks as if he's going to be as great a scientist as his dad.

Kyrano looks after the house and compound on Tracy island, and his wife **Onaha** does the cooking. Their watersports-mad daughter is called **Tintin**.

At fourteen, **Alan** is the youngest of Jeff Tracy's sons. His one aim in life is to join his brothers as a member of the International Rescue team. It sometimes feels a long way off, but it may happen sooner than he thinks ...

AND ENEMIES

The Hood is the name used by master criminal Trangh Belagant. He believes that International Rescue once left him to die and has sworn to take his revenge by destroying the organization. To help him, he has learned amazing mental powers. The Hood may not always speak out loud, but when he looks into your eyes you know exactly what he's saying!

Transom is the Hood's scientific officer. She wears a black leather catsuit, she's a fearsome fighter – and she has very bad teeth!

Mullion is the Hood's main muscle man. He's very dangerous because he's strong, ruthless – and he always does exactly as his boss tells him, whatever it may be.

17

IR SKILLS ASSESSMENT:1

Do you have what it takes to be part of International Rescue? Test your skills, knowledge and response times, then check your International Rescue Skills Rating.

You have a maximum of 3 minutes to answer true or false to all 12 questions.

All the answers can be found in this annual.

		TRUE	FALSE
1.	Lady Penelope's surname is Clayton-Wall.		✓
2.	John Tracy pilots Thunderbird 5.	✓	
3.	Jeff Tracy has 6 sons.		✓
4.	Tintin is the daughter of Onaha and Kyrano.	✓	
5.	Thunderbird 4 is a one-man submarine.	✓	✓
6.	Parker used to be a boxer.	✓	

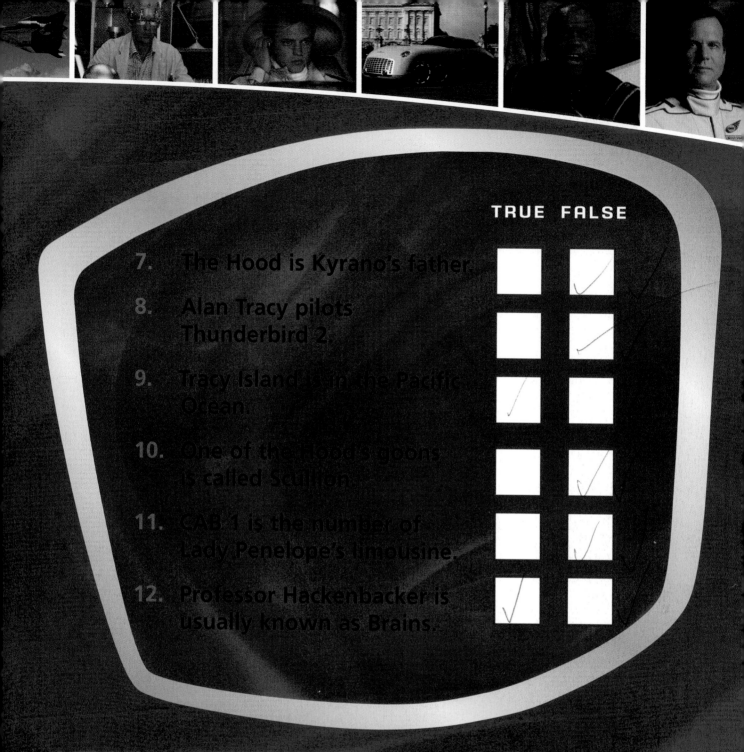

TRUE   FALSE

7.   The Hood is Kyrano's father.

8.   Alan Tracy pilots
     Thunderbird 2.

9.   Tracy Island is in the Pacific
     Ocean.

10. One of the Hood's goons
     is called Scullion.

11. CAB 1 is the number of
     Lady Penelope's limousine.

12. Professor Hackenbacker is
     usually known as Brains.

INTERNATIONAL RESCUE SKILLS RATING

12 points   Excellent. You're in! When can you join the team?
10-11 points   Very, very good. With just a little more training, who knows?
7-9 points   Good result. Why not brush up your knowledge and try again?
4-6 points   Very average. Call yourself an International Rescue fan?
Less than 4 points   Oh dear! Ever thought of a career as a dog walker?

Answers: 1. false, it's Creighton-Ward. 2. true. 3. false, he has 5. 4. true. 5. true. 6. true. 7. false, he's his brother. 8. false, Virgil does. 9. true. 10. false, his name is Mullion. 11. false, it's FAB 1. 12. true

FAB 1

NAME:	FAB 1
OWNER:	Lady Penelope Creighton-Ward
DRIVER:	Parker
TECHNICAL DATA:	
colour:	pink
weight:	1.4 tons
length:	7 metres
width:	2 metres
Engine:	Ford V6
land speed:	100 miles per hour plus
sea speed:	50 knots

Lady Penelope Creighton-Ward is the perfect undercover agent: clever, cool and calm, with a will of steel. She's a martial arts expert too.

Parker is Lady Penelope's chauffeur and gets to drive the most FABulous car in the world. He was once a top boxer, so he can really handle himself.

ROLE:

FAB 1 is no ordinary car. Lady Penelope's limousine is low, sleek, smooth and fast, and is packed with gizmos and high-tech gadgets. It has six wheels and is fitted with a bulletproof glass canopy roof. It transforms so that it can fly as a jet plane and is able to travel on water too, as a sleek catamaran. As Lady Penelope says, FAB 1 is the only way to travel.

Oh, and one more thing. FAB 1 is bright, bright pink ...

CHAPTER 2

A long, black submarine powered its way beneath the surface of the Pacific Ocean. It had been built using advanced stealth technology and was all but invisible to the naked eye, to the world's super powers – and even to International Rescue …

A green light pulsed on the tracking screen of the submarine as a man sat hunched over the control console. This was the Hood, master criminal and the Thunderbirds' unknown enemy. He was concentrating hard, his eyes totally focused on the screen and the Thunderbirds craft that filled it. The green light was a signal he was picking up, its origins in the chemical that the rig worker had fired, and which was now embedded in the fuselage of Thunderbird 1. It would enable him to track the huge rocket ship as it powered back to its secret base …

The Hood watched as Thunderbird 1 streaked away from the west coast of America and over the Pacific Ocean. He smiled a small smile – a very small smile. "Follow its flight path," he ordered.

Silent and deadly, the submarine cut through the ocean like a shark tracking its prey.

• • •

"We are now on final approach to Tracy Island," said Parker, as FAB 1 arced low over the ocean. "And radar indicates that we have company."

There was a powerful blast and a loud roaring sound. FAB 1 shook as Thunderbirds 1 and 2 swooped alongside just long enough for Jeff Tracy to give his son a thumbs-up sign. Then they peeled away and surged for home.

Alan sighed. He wished he was on board one of the Thunderbirds instead of just watching them. It wasn't fair that he was always left out.

His mood was lifted by the sight of Tracy Island up ahead, its steep sides covered in dense green jungle, a central peak piercing the sky, and its edges fringed with white, sandy beaches.

He glanced at the modern house made of glass and steel that stood near the shore as FAB 1 taxied past the palm trees that lined the runway. This was home: Tracy Island, a tropical paradise. But it was also the secret headquarters of International Rescue.

By the time they got to the house, the Thunderbirds were stowed in their underground hangars and Jeff and his family were in the kitchen.

The housekeeper, Onaha, was making dinner and Jeff was chatting with Fermat's father, who everyone called Brains. There was a good reason for this: he was the technical wizard who kept the Thunderbirds flying.

Alan's older brothers, Scott, Virgil and Gordon, were chatting about a mission.

One son was missing: John remained out in space on Thunderbird 5, the vast space station that monitored the globe using its wide array of state-of-the-art communications equipment.

If there was a disaster or emergency anywhere on the planet, Thunderbird 5 would detect and report on it.

When they were all seated at the table, Alan couldn't wait to talk to his brothers about the mission.

"Did you readjust the flaps?" he asked Scott.

"Sure. First thing I did," said Scott.

"Try to keep up, Alan!" said Gordon, teasing his little brother.

"Yeah, don't you have homework or something?" asked Virgil.

"That's enough, boys," said Jeff. He knew they were joking – but Alan didn't.

"I'm not hungry!" Alan said, pushing his plate away. "Come on, Fermat!"

By the time Jeff got outside, they were gone.

Jeff looked everywhere for the boys – everywhere except the cockpit of Thunderbird 1, where Alan and Fermat sat at the controls. "Run pre-flight checks."

"Hydraulic systems green," said Fermat.

"Commence main engine sequence," said Alan, reaching for a switch.

"No, Alan, that's the …" said Fermat, but it was too late. The cockpit lit up, dials and instrument panels glowed, lights flashed and the onboard computer hummed and whirred into life.

Jeff Tracy's face appeared on the main monitor. "Alan. My office. NOW."

The two boys climbed down from the cockpit with a feeling of dread. This was not a good start to the holiday. As he passed the fuselage, Fermat noticed something unusual: a glittering patch with a strange sheen. He wasn't an expert, but he knew the vehicle was always spotless. He had a feeling that whatever was there shouldn't be there, so he pulled a swab from his pocket and took a sample. It looked like a gallium compound. He didn't know what it was doing there – but he would find out …

•••

Jeff was waiting when Alan burst into his office. "I know you're mad, but we found this …" said Alan.

"No excuses," said Jeff. "You're grounded. You know you're not allowed in the cockpit. You're not ready."

"But I had it under control …"

"Really? You started a Thunderbird without the anti-detection shield! You could have revealed our location. You put everyone in danger. If you want to be part of the team, you have to follow the rules. Understand?"

Alan was angry. "Oh, I understand," he said. "I understand that you don't want me to be a Thunderbird!" and he ran from the office.

•••

Not too far away, hidden under the surface of the Pacific Ocean, one of the Hood's goons, Mullion, peered through the periscope of the submarine. He was the fake 'oil rig worker' who had fired the gallium compound at Thunderbird 1.

"The island is in sight," he reported.

"Very good," said the Hood, pressing a button. "Transom, I need you."

A young woman in a black leather catsuit appeared. "We have a positive visual," she reported. "Missiles are armed and ready. Should I target the buildings?"

"Why destroy what will soon be mine?" asked the Hood. "I have been taught to use an opponent's strength against him. It would be almost impossible to force the Thunderbirds to leave the island. But it takes no effort at all to LET them go. Their purpose is rescue. We need to give them a victim." He paused. "Commence target triangulation of Thunderbird 5."

"Target locked," said Transom.

"Fire!" whispered the Hood.

• • •

The missile from the Hood's submarine burst from the sea unseen. The stealth properties of the weapon made it invisible to electronic detection. Not even radar could spot it.

The missile arced high into the sky and its wings unfolded. Then, as it came closer to its target, it started to spin, faster and faster, until the wings were just a blur.

It soared higher and higher, into the upper atmosphere, moving closer

and closer to its target – Thunderbird 5.

When the weapon made contact with the mighty space station, it tore through its outer ring, leaving an ugly hole in the fuselage. The whole space station rocked under the impact and John Tracy was thrown from his seat, slamming against an instrument panel. Emergency lights flashed and alarms blared, but it was too late …

John struggled to his feet and looked at the monitor screens. It was all bad news:

HULL BREACH … LOSS OF ATMOSPHERE … AUTO-REPAIR SYSTEMS NEGATIVE …

There was worse to come: sparks fizzed from the control panels and black smoke billowed. Computer screens flashed and crackled then, one by one, the computers exploded, engulfing the control room in smoke and flames!

John lost no time. He picked himself up from the floor and hit the communications equipment: "Thunderbird 5 to Tracy Island," he reported.

"EMERGENCY! MAYDAY! MAYDAY!"

continued on page 30 …

IR SKILLS ASSESSMENT: 2

So you have what it takes to be part of International Rescue? Test your knowledge and response times, then check your International Rescue Skills Rating.

You have a maximum of 5 minutes to discover the identities of 5 people and 5 vehicles from the clues.

3. I work for the Hood.
I dress in a black leather catsuit.
I have very bad teeth.
Who am I?

Mullion Transom

1. I am an undercover agent.
I travel in FAB 1.
I adore all things pink.
Who am I?

Penny

4. I attend Wharton Academy.
I am fourteen years old.
My best friend is called Fermat.
Who am I?

Alan

2. I am an ex-astronaut.
I pilot Thunderbird 3.
I have 5 sons.
Who am I?

Jeff

5. I am married to Onaha.
I have a daughter called Tintin.
I look after the Tracy compound.
Who am I?

Kyrano

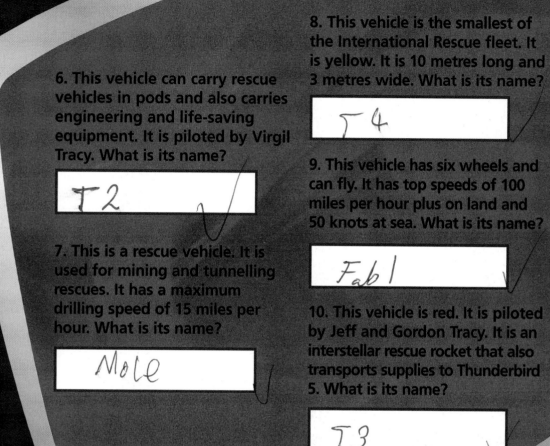

6. This vehicle can carry rescue vehicles in pods and also carries engineering and life-saving equipment. It is piloted by Virgil Tracy. What is its name?

T2 ✓

7. This is a rescue vehicle. It is used for mining and tunnelling rescues. It has a maximum drilling speed of 15 miles per hour. What is its name?

Mole ✓

8. This vehicle is the smallest of the International Rescue fleet. It is yellow. It is 10 metres long and 3 metres wide. What is its name?

T4 ✓

9. This vehicle has six wheels and can fly. It has top speeds of 100 miles per hour plus on land and 50 knots at sea. What is its name?

Fab1 ✓

10. This vehicle is red. It is piloted by Jeff and Gordon Tracy. It is an interstellar rescue rocket that also transports supplies to Thunderbird 5. What is its name?

T3 ✓

INTERNATIONAL RESCUE SKILLS RATING

10 points   Well done! You feel at home in any vehicle!
7-9 points   What a rescuer! You are almost ready to take off!
6-8 points   So-so! Call yourself an International Rescue recruit?
5 points or less   You need to develop your skills. Why not read the annual and try again?

CHAPTER 3

Fermat finally got the chance to tell his father about the sample he had taken from Thunderbird 1's nose cone.

"I think it's some sort of gallium compound."

"Gallium? That could be important," said Brains. "Let's check it out."

But before they could do that, the emergency signal sounded and they raced to Jeff's office.

"Switching to command and control centre," said Brains, and the office transformed into the headquarters of International Rescue.

The desk swung into the floor and was replaced by an ultra-high-tech command console. Pictures on the walls became giant monitor screens. Banks of computers rose from the floor and descended from the ceiling. Finally, blast-proof steel shutters slid shut across the windows.

Jeff Tracy and his three older sons, Virgil, Scott and Gordon, rushed in and stood in front of their pictures, which covered one wall.

"Major damage to Thunderbird 5," Brains told them. "Possible meteor strike."

"Thunderbirds are GO!" said Jeff and, as he spoke, the pictures morphed into images of the Tracys in International Rescue uniforms.

Then the wall flipped back and they slid down the launch chutes to the Thunderbirds hangar.

Seconds later, Jeff, Virgil, Scott and Gordon blasted off in Thunderbird 3 on a mission with a difference: they were going to rescue John!

•••

Alan and Tintin were on the beach when Fermat told them that Thunderbird 5 had been hit. "John's in trouble. Your dad and brothers have gone to help."

Alan's eyes were wide with shock, but his voice was calm. "International Rescue can handle this."

As he spoke, the sea behind them churned and a huge black submarine broke through the surface and headed straight for the beach.

Alan's eyes opened wider. "RUN!"

On board, the Hood smiled. "Cut them off."

Transom threw a switch. "Communications blackout activated," she said. "They won't know what hit them."

"Until we tell them," said the Hood.

•••

In the far reaches of space, Jeff Tracy had a visual on Thunderbird 5. But what he saw was not good. Debris from the huge impact hung in space around the damaged space station as it trembled and shook, its orbit destroyed.

He heard John's voice. "I'm losing all power."

"We're coming," said Jeff, guiding the rocket towards the docking port.

There was more bad news. "Thunderbird 5's gyros aren't working," said Scott. "The docking computer can't get a lock."

"Then we'll have to do this the old-fashioned way," said Jeff. "Hang on, boys."

He guided Thunderbird 3 with the control stick, lining up the ships' docking ports, and moved in, slowly, slowly …

For a heart-stopping second, it seemed that the ships would collide, but at the last moment, Jeff pulled back on the stick and turned.

"Now, Scott!" he barked.

Scott activated the docking mechanism and, with a clunk, the airlocks met, linked – and sealed.

Seconds later, the doors linking the ships opened, and Jeff and his sons sprinted into Thunderbird 5.

They saw smoke and flames in every direction. Emergency lights flashed in the darkness and alarms blared.

Suddenly, John appeared out of the blackness. "Am I glad to see you guys!"

•••

On Tracy Island, Alan, Fermat and Tintin watched as the Hood and his team strode towards the Tracy compound.

"How did they find the island?" Alan whispered.

"That stuff we found on the side of the ship might have some kind of transmitting capability," said Fermat. "It may have led them here."

"We need to warn the others," said Tintin.

"Dad's in the control room," said Fermat. "But how do we get there? We're cut off from the complex."

Alan's brain raced. "The vents!" he said, pointing to a big intake, and they heaved off the cover.

•••

In the control room, Brains saw the intruders on the security monitors, touched a switch, and the room transformed back into Jeff Tracy's office.

Then he tried to reach the Thunderbirds. "Jeff ... Scott ... come in!"

As Brains spoke, a huge explosion shook the steel door and Mullion charged into the room, knocking him to the floor.

"Who are you?" Brains asked, as the Hood entered.

"More importantly, who are the Thunderbirds?" asked the Hood, as his eyes rested on the pictures of the Tracys. "Ah, Jeff Tracy, billionaire ex-astronaut. I should have guessed."

Transom pulled out a scanner. "The command control system is here, sir," she said. "It's a fingerprint recognition system."

"Please activate the control switch," said the Hood.

Brains shook his head. "Never."

The Hood was a master of a strange form of mind control. He stared hard at Brains, his eyes flashing and pulsing, the pupils growing larger, then smaller. "Activate the control switch," he repeated.

Brains stared back. He tried to fight off the evil in the Hood's eyes, but his body jerked and he walked to the desk. He tried to stop his fingers doing what the Hood wanted them to, but it was no good. He flicked a switch and out slid a hand-recognition plate.

Unable to stop himself, he pressed his hand flat on the plate and the room transformed into the headquarters of International Rescue.

Transom smiled. "We have control!"

• • •

On Thunderbird 5, Jeff made a decision. "Back to Thunderbird 3," he ordered. "NOW!"

In the airlock corridor, Scott punched the keypad, but nothing happened. "The locking mechanism's jammed!" he yelled.

Lights flared then dimmed as the power surged and failed. Then a viewing screen flickered into life and the Hood appeared.

"Attention, Thunderbird 5," he said calmly. "I have taken over. You are no longer in control of your operational systems."

"Who are you?" asked Jeff.

"How rude of me," said the Hood. "You can call me the Hood, Mr Tracy. I am here so that you can see me destroy in hours what it took you years to build. I am going to use the Thunderbirds to rob the world's largest banks ... starting with the Bank of England. The world will be in chaos as a result – and the Thunderbirds will be responsible."

"But the Thunderbirds exist to save lives," said Jeff.

The Hood's eyes flashed. "Yes, and you saved the life of Kyrano – my brother. But you left me to die. For that you must suffer."

With that, the Hood's face disappeared, leaving Jeff and his sons to wonder how they were going to stop his evil plan.

Scott and Gordon worked hard – and fast. "We've wired in the emergency batteries," said Scott.

"How long will it buy us?" asked Jeff.

"Four hours – max."

continued on page 46 ...

THE FLEET

name:	Thunderbird 1
pilot:	scott tracy

technical data:

type:	supersonic spearhead reconnaissance rocket
colour:	silver grey, with blue and yellow detailing and red nose cone
weight:	140 tons
length:	25 metres
wingspan:	9 metres
maximum altitude:	150,000 feet
diameter:	4 metres
maximum speed:	15,000 miles per hour

ROLE:
Thunderbird 1 is the International Rescue reconnaissance rocket. It is specially designed to reach disaster or emergency zones in the shortest possible time and is always first on the scene. There it assesses the situation and serves in rescues. Ultra-high-speed, it is also supremely manoeuvrable.

THUNDERBIRDS

THE FLEET

NAME: thunderbird 2

PILOT: virgil tracy

TECHNICAL DATA:

type: heavy duty freighter

colour: green, with red and
                             yellow detailing

weight: 406 tons

length: 45 metres

wingspan: 33 metres

cruising speed: 2,000 miles
                             per hour

maximum altitude: 150,000 feet

main body diameter: 18 metres

maximum speed: 5,000 miles
                             per hour

ROLE:

Thunderbird 2 is the workhorse of the International Rescue fleet. Thanks to its supreme power and strength, the massive green turtle-shaped leviathan carries essential heavy-duty engineering and life-saving equipment. It also carries Thunderbird 4, and the Mole, Firefly and Thunderizer rescue vehicles, in pods.

THUNDERBIRDS

THE FLEET

NAME: Thunderbird 3

PILOTS: Jeff Tracy
Gordon Tracy

TECHNICAL DATA:

type: interstellar rescue rocket

colour: red, with silver grey detailing

weight: 562 tons

length: 58 metres

main body diameter: 7 metres

maximum speed: 5,000 miles per hour

ROLE:

Thunderbird 3 is International Rescue's space rescue and shuttle craft. It is designed to speed between Earth and space, and is used for extra-orbital missions. It is also used as a link to Thunderbird 5, transporting supplies and equipment to the space station.

THUNDERBIRDS™

THE FLEET

NAME: Thunderbird 4

PILOT: Alan Tracy

TECHNICAL DATA:

type: one-man mini submarine

colour: yellow

length: 9 metres

width: 3 metres

launch speed: 80 miles per hour

surface cruising speed: 40 knots

underwater speed: 160 knots

maximum operating depth: 30,000 feet

ROLE:

Thunderbird 4 is the International Rescue underwater emergency, rescue, repair and reconnaissance vehicle. It has many uses, from daring marine rescues to removing obstacles and objects from the ocean floor, and gathering deep-sea eco samples. It is the smallest of the fleet and is carried onboard Thunderbird 2.

THE FLEET

NAME: Thunderbird 5

PILOT: John Tracy

TECHNICAL DATA:

type: orbiting space station

colour: bronze and silver grey,
                       with red and yellow detailing

weight: 976 tons

height: 82 metres

diameter: 61 metres

power source: atomic batteries

reception range: 100,000,000 miles

orbit: 22,400 miles above
                       the pacific ocean

ROLE:

Thunderbird 5 is the International Rescue communications satellite. Operating in permanent geo-stationary orbit around the Earth, its vital role is at the hub of the secret organization's communications network. It provides immediate data on rescue and emergency situations all around the world as well as constantly monitoring Tracy Island and Thunderbirds 1, 2, 3 and 4.

CHAPTER 4

Back on Tracy Island, Alan, Fermat and Tintin were hiding in the ventilation duct behind the International Rescue control room.

Alan was trying to hear what was going on. His ear was pressed hard to the wall when Fermat sneezed. Seconds later Mullion's huge fist slammed through the picture screen next to them. He took hold of Alan's shirt and was pulling him towards the control room when Tintin bit his hand – hard.

Mullion yelled in pain, let go, and Alan, Fermat and Tintin dived into the nearby launch chutes. They shot down the slide towards the underground hangar where the remaining Thunderbirds waited ...

In the control room, the Hood sneered at Mullion. "So, the island is not as secure as you thought. There are children here. Children!"

Transom brought up a picture on the monitor. "They're in the Thunderbird 2 silo," she said.

The Hood nodded. "Seal them in."

Far below, the blast doors leading to Thunderbird 3's hangar slid shut.

"We're trapped!" said Tintin.

"If we can get to Thunderbird 1's silo, we can escape through the service tunnel," said Fermat.

"OK. I'll handle the door. You use the Firefly to take care of those goons," said Alan, pointing to the mighty eight-wheeled firefighting rescue truck.

Fermat and Tintin ran to the Firefly. As they climbed on board, the lift doors opened. "Here they come!" yelled Tintin, as Fermat gunned the engine and they lurched forward.

Alan slipped into an equipment pod and emerged at the controls of the Thunderizer, another rescue machine. It was used to blast through buildings without harming any people trapped inside – but Alan had other ideas for it.

On the Firefly, Tintin aimed the mighty foam cannon at Mullion and his men, and the force blasted them back into the lift.

Then it was Alan's turn. He turned the Thunderizer's cannon on the door into Thunderbird 1's hangar, and a ball of green energy particles blew a hole right through it.

"Come on!" Alan yelled, running for the service tunnel door.

He punched in the entry code. "That should just about ..." he said, then stopped in mid-sentence.

Someone was waiting on the other side of the glass door – the Hood.

Alan's eyes were drawn to the Hood's evil gaze, and locked there. He couldn't hear the Hood's words, but somehow he knew exactly what he was saying. "You know what your father did to me, don't you? He left me to die."

Alan's eyes were still locked on the Hood's, whose lips did not move, but whose instructions were very clear. "Open the door, Alan."

Alan knew he had to resist, but it took all his willpower. Finally he tore his eyes away from the Hood's and turned from the door.

The three teens backed up to the base of Thunderbird 1.

Alan took out his techno-slingshot and fired a stone that hit a button on the wall. The doors underneath Thunderbird 1 opened and Alan, Fermat and Tintin dropped inside …

Mullion knew what had to be done. He had an order for Transom. "Fire up the engines on Thunderbird 1."

Sliding down the tube, the teens heard the blast of the mighty engines coming to life behind them. A wall of fire was heading their way.

Suddenly, the chute dropped away from under them and they plunged down, hitting the waters of the Pacific Ocean – hard. Then the sea closed in over their heads …

Alan and Tintin soon burst to the surface in a hidden lagoon.

"Where's Fermat?" asked Alan.

Tintin knew he couldn't swim, so she dived back under and emerged towing Fermat. Then they clambered back on to dry land.

"The Hood must have overridden Thunderbird 5's systems using the main computer in the control room," said Alan. "All we need to do is re-programme it."

"I have an idea," said Fermat. "Data and commands from the island are sent to Thunderbird 5 by satellite, so if we could hack into that, we can give control back to Thunderbird 5."

"Let's do it," said Alan. "Come on."

Tintin led the way, but the climb to the satellite station was long and hard. "OK," she said after a steep patch. "Take five." Then her eyes opened wide. Very wide. "Alan, don't move!"

"What is it?" asked Alan.

"Black scorpion, on your shoulder," said Tintin.

"Its venom is fatal," added Fermat.

"I'll deal with it," said Tintin, and she stared hard at the scorpion as Alan and Fermat held their breath.

Then her eyes flashed – and the scorpion flew off Alan's shoulder.

"How did you do that?" asked Alan.

"Let's get going," said Tintin. She didn't say another word, but the look she gave Alan made her message clear: don't ask.

Alan looked at Fermat, shrugged, and set off after her.

 The Hood was still in the control room. "Pick out the equipment you need to get into the banks and load it into Thunderbird 2," he told Mullion.

•••

Meanwhile, far away, Lady Penelope was enjoying a long bubble bath. She had discovered that one of the rescued oil workers was an imposter and brought up pictures of Mullion and Transom on the viewscreen by the bath.

"They work for the Hood, real name Trangh Belagant," she read. "He was assumed dead when his diamond mine collapsed. The Thunderbirds rescued the workers, including his brother – Kyrano!"

Lady Penelope reached for a towel. "I think the Thunderbirds may be in a spot of trouble," she said. "PARKER!"

Within minutes, FAB 1 was heading back to Tracy Island, where Fermat had finally managed to re-establish communication links with Thunderbird 5.

"Dad, we're going to give control of Thunderbird 5 back to you," said Alan.

But before they could, Transom traced the signal – and jammed it.
Jeff's face faded from the screen.

"They know where we are!" said Fermat, as an armoured four-wheel buggy with Mullion at the controls approached at speed.

"We have to go!" said Tintin.

They careered off down the mountainside on an old powered hover-sled, with Alan at the controls and Tintin and Fermat in the trailer.

Mullion was right behind and gaining on them, so Alan steered the sled through a narrow gap in the rocks that the buggy would never fit through, then glanced back. "NO!" he whispered. The trailer lay on its side on the far side of the rocks, and Mullion was closing in on Fermat and Tintin!

Alan gunned the sled's engines and shot off down the mountain. Now he was on his own ...

continued on page 56 ...

RESCUE VEHICLES

Name: THE FIREFLY

Technical Data:

colour: yellow and red

weight (including transporter): 8 tons

length (including transporter): 7.5 metres

width: 4 metres

height: 8 metres

maximum speed: 25 miles per hour

Role:

The Firefly is mainly used as a fire-fighting bulldozer. It has powerful cannons mounted on top which fire huge amounts of high-pressure foam produced in special pods. The foam is very effective in extinguishing fires. Because the Firefly is used in very dangerous situations, the driver sits in a special insulated cab which is lined with heatproof and flame-resistant materials.

NAME: THE MOLE

TECHNICAL DATA:

colour: silver grey, yellow and red

weight (including transporter): 12 tons

length (including transporter): 18 metres

width: 3.5 metres

maximum drilling speed: 15 miles per hour

ROLE: Using the very latest mining and tunnelling technology, the Mole is able to tunnel to any rescue site, even into the Earth's core if necessary. It is equipped with a tungsten carbide cutter head and diamond-tipped blades, which can cut and grind the hardest rock into smaller stones and fragments. It normally travels on its own transporter, but can also be carried in a pod on Thunderbird 2.

NAME: THE THUNDERIZER

TECHNICAL DATA:

colour: red and yellow

weight (including transporter): 10 tons

length (including transporter): 7 metres

width: 3 metres

height: 4 metres

maximum speed: 20 miles per hour

ROLE: The Thunderizer is a massive laser cannon mounted on a powerful base vehicle powered by a high-performance engine. Its caterpillar tracks mean that it can travel over the roughest terrain. When fired, the laser cannon releases intense beams of charged particles, a single one of which can blow a hole in concrete or metal up to 2 metres thick.

IR SKILLS ASSESSMENT: 3

Do you have the visual skills all
International Rescue personnel need?
Test your performance against the clock, then
check your International Rescue Skills Rating.

You have 5 minutes to identify 8 things that are different
in picture 2. Circle them, or write a list.

Score 1 point for each change you identify within the time limit.

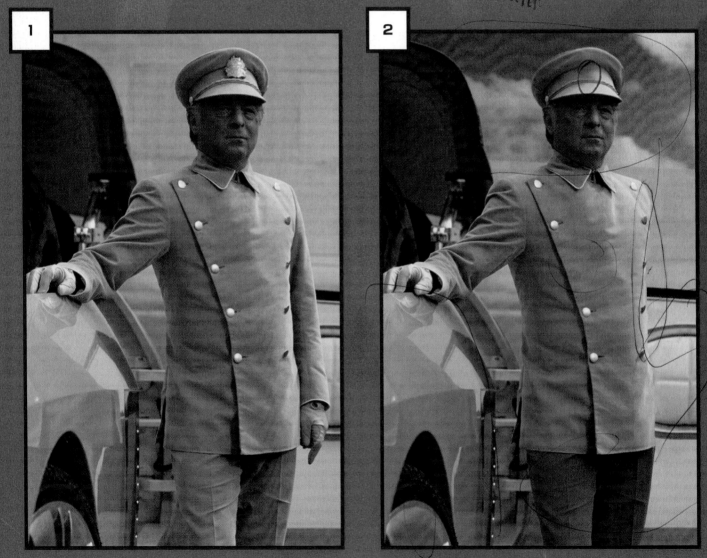

1

2

Answers:
1. The badge on Parker's hat is missing;
2. FAB 1 has changed from pink to green; 3. Parker's left arm is missing;
4. Parker's trousers are brown; 5. Parker's jacket has a button missing; 6. FAB 1's open door is pink;
7. There is sky in the background instead of wall; 8. The grooves on FAB 1's wheel are missing.

.... points

54

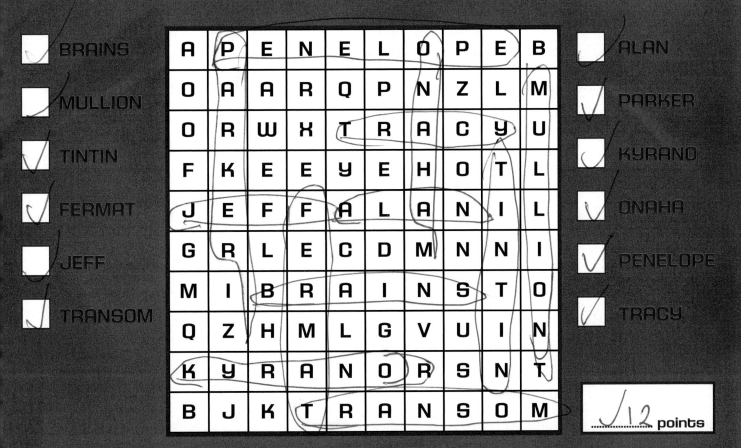

The Thunderbirds need to be able to identify friends and enemies, and they need to do it fast.

Can you find these 12 names in the word square, and tick each name as you find it? They are spelled out from top to bottom and from left to right.

You have 5 minutes to do the task. Score 1 point for each name you tick.

☑ BRAINS

☑ MULLION

☑ TINTIN

☑ FERMAT

☑ JEFF

☑ TRANSOM

A	P	E	N	E	L	O	P	E	B
O	A	A	R	Q	P	N	Z	L	M
O	R	W	X	T	R	A	C	Y	U
F	K	E	E	Y	E	H	O	T	L
J	E	F	F	A	L	A	N	I	L
G	R	L	E	C	D	M	N	N	I
M	I	B	R	A	I	N	S	T	O
Q	Z	H	M	L	G	V	U	I	N
K	Y	R	A	N	O	R	S	N	T
B	J	K	T	R	A	N	S	O	M

☑ ALAN

☑ PARKER

☑ KYRANO

☑ ONAHA

☑ PENELOPE

☑ TRACY

☑ 12 points

Add your points from pages 54 and 55 and check your rating.

INTERNATIONAL RESCUE SKILLS RATING

20 points	When can you collect your uniform?
15-19 points	Very good. Why not do some extra training?
10-14 points	Well done. Good result.
5-9 points	Must try harder.
Less than 5 points	This is not good, is it?

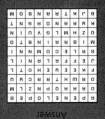

Answer

CHAPTER 5

The Tracy home freezer was large, dark, very cold and the perfect place to keep prisoners – which is how Fermat and Tintin came to be reunited with Brains, Onaha and Kyrano.

While they shivered inside, FAB 1 was approaching Tracy Island. With the peak of the volcano in sight, Parker switched to aqua mode and the flying car's wings retracted, then the nose reshaped into the prow of a speedboat. Two large fins appeared from the car's sides, transforming it into a sleek pink catamaran.

But the supercar's approach had been seen and, as it drew close to the shore, a torpedo was fired from the Hood's submarine, forcing Lady Penelope and Parker to abandon ship before it hit and make their way to the shore in a life-raft. A bright pink life-raft!

•••

Out in space, Thunderbirds 3 and 5 drifted into the Earth's atmosphere.

"Re-entry in thirty-seven minutes," reported Virgil.

"But our oxygen won't last that long," said Scott. "It's hopeless."

"No, it's not hopeless when we've got people on the ground working for us," said Jeff.

"Alan?" said John. "He's just a kid."

"But he's a TRACY kid," said John. "He'll think of something."

• • •

Back on Earth, Alan was wishing he COULD think of something, when he saw Lady Penelope and Parker heading for the shore and raced to meet them.

But Mullion got to them first. "Be warned, I know judo and tae kwon do," he said.

Lady Penelope smiled. "And I know Parker."

The chauffeur stepped forward, punched Mullion on the nose and was about to hit him again when Transom and the Hood arrived. Even Parker was no match for two goons at once, so it was left to Lady Penelope to deal with them.

She did so in her own unique style, with a series of flips, turns and kicks that left Mullion and Transom in a senseless heap.

She was fighting with the Hood when Mullion came to, grabbed her from behind and tied her up. Then Transom recovered and tied up Parker.

The Hood smiled and nodded to Mullion, who kicked out at Parker.

"You can make him stop ... Alan," said the Hood.

Alan was hiding in the bushes. His eyes opened wide and his blood ran cold. How did the Hood know he was there?

Mullion kicked Parker again and Alan stepped into the open. "Stop!"

The Hood smiled again. "Put them in the freezer with the others."

•••

Minutes later, the Hood and his gang were aboard Thunderbird 2. "Ready for take-off," said Transom.

"Estimated time of arrival in London?" asked the Hood.

"Under an hour," replied Mullion. "Bank of England, here we come!"

Thunderbird 2's engines roared into life and the green monster took off into the skies.

•••

In the freezer, Alan and the others knew just how little time they had. Out in space on Thunderbird 5, Jeff and his sons had very little oxygen left. When it ran out, they would die …

"We have to get to the control room!" said Alan. "But how?"

Lady Penelope knew. She did a high kick and the stiletto heel of her shoe sliced through an icicle, which dropped, cutting through the ropes around Parker's wrists.

He used the icicle to free the others, then forced the door and they raced to the control room. What they saw on the monitors was not good. Jeff and the team lay still and seemingly lifeless on the out of control space station.

"There's no time to lose!" cried Alan, as Brains and Fermat hit the computer controls and tried to get a response from the ship.

"Twenty seconds to re-entry!" said Fermat.

Brains yelled into the mic. "WAKE UP!"

Jeff's eyes flickered, then opened.

"Confirm access protocol," said Fermat.

"Confirmed!" gasped John.

"You have control!" said Brains.

Jeff took the space station's control stick and moved it forward. As he did so, massive retro-rockets fired as the seconds to re-entry counted down on the screen:

5 ... 4 ... 3 ... 2 ... 1 ...

"We were too late," said Tintin.

But then they heard Jeff's voice again. "F A B, Brains. We're good to go."

The control room erupted in cheers and whoops as Jeff reported in again. "We're fine, but there's still work to do. Where's the Hood?"

"Heading for London," said Brains. "In Thunderbird 2."

"With the Mole," added Alan. "Let me go after him, Dad."

"It's too dangerous," said Jeff.

"You know I can do this," said Alan. Then he moved to where Lady Penelope, Tintin and Fermat were standing. "Correction. WE can do this."

Jeff was silent for a while, then he spoke. "OK, we'll meet you there. Thunderbirds are go!"

Lady Penelope and the teens stood against the picture wall and, as Brains hit a switch, the wall gave way and they flew down the launch tube leading to Thunderbird 1.

They changed into International Rescue uniforms and climbed into the cockpit, with Alan and Fermat at the controls.

This time the take-off routine was for real. The engines fired, the hangar roof slid aside and Alan and Fermat pushed the levers forward. Seconds later, Thunderbird 1 soared into the clouds, leaving behind a trail of fire.

Alan looked at Fermat. "We can stop him if we get there in time."

Fermat nodded. "Maximum thrust!" he said as a mighty boom sounded and they smashed through the sound barrier.

Jeff's voice came on the radio. "Thunderbird 3 released. We're on our way to London."

Alan smiled. "F A B."

•••

Minutes later, Thunderbird 2 was over London. It flew low under Tower Bridge, skimming the waters of the River Thames and shattering a thousand windows in tall buildings on the banks.

Passers-by pointed and stared. So did passengers on the new monorail, who gazed up as the huge shadow passed over them.

But excitement turned to horror as the mighty craft dropped from the sky, landing on an ice-cream van and squashing it flat! People gasped in shock. What were the Thunderbirds doing?

They soon found out. Thunderbird 2 rose up and a speaker hummed and crackled.

"A change is announced," said Mullion. "The Thunderbirds are no longer here to rescue. We are here to destroy."

Then the door of the pod opened and the mighty Mole rescue drilling vehicle rolled out, a huge cone like a giant screw on its nose.

People ran, screaming, as it began boring into the ground.

Inside the Mole's cockpit the Hood spoke. "Set a course for the Bank of England."

"Sir, that course will cut the monorail's supports," said Transom. "Shall I change course?"

"No, stay on course," said the Hood.

"But we'll cause a major disaster," said Transom.

"No we won't," said the Hood, smiling. "But the Thunderbirds will!"

As he spoke, the Mole drilled deeper and the monorail started to creak, crumple and collapse. The rail line snapped and concrete pillars toppled into the river. The monorail carriage was left hanging from a single cable, dangling just above the surface of the river, as passengers screamed in panic.

Just then, Thunderbird 1 landed. "We need to take back Thunderbird 2," said Alan. "Come on!"

Alan, Fermat and Tintin raced to the cockpit and fired the engines.

"What do we do?" asked Fermat. "Stop the Hood, or try to rescue these people?"

"We're the Thunderbirds," said Alan. "Our duty is to save these people."

He gunned the engines and Thunderbird 2 lifted off towards the monorail. Fermat fired a grappling rocket trailing a cable behind it, which locked on to the tracks. Slowly, Thunderbird 2 rose up and the cable began to pull the rail straight.

But suddenly a mighty crack split the rail in two. The carriage rolled and started to sink into the dark river …

continued on page 64 …

IR SKILLS ASSESSMENT: 4

Technical skills aren't the only ones needed by the International Rescue team. They need good creative skills, too.

Put yours to the test by copying this picture of Thunderbird 2 section by section, then colour your drawing. You have 15 minutes to complete the task.

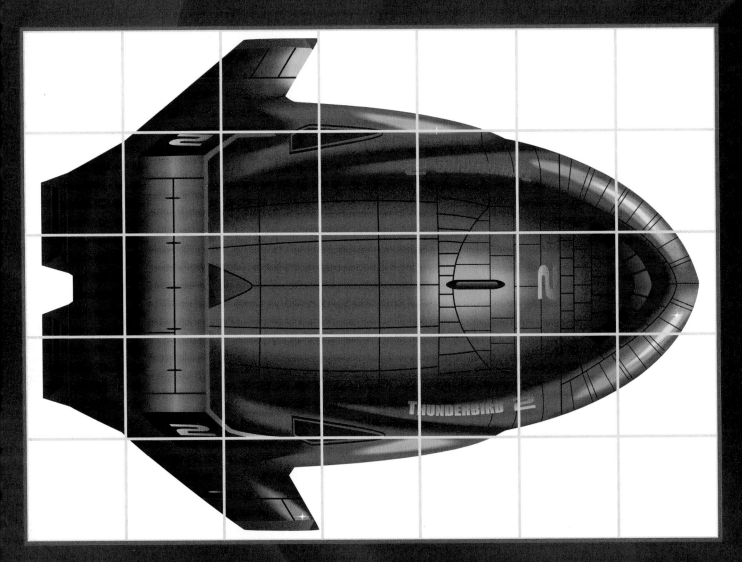

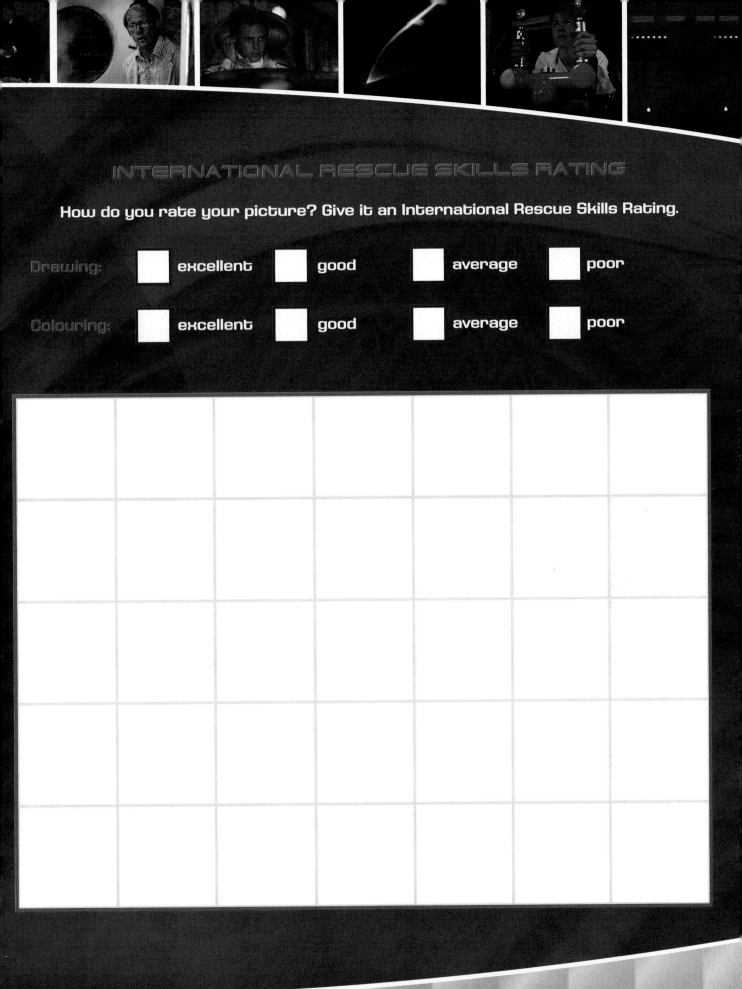

INTERNATIONAL RESCUE SKILLS RATING

How do you rate your picture? Give it an International Rescue Skills Rating.

Drawing: ☐ excellent ☐ good ☐ average ☐ poor

Colouring: ☐ excellent ☐ good ☐ average ☐ poor

CHAPTER 6

As the monorail carriage disappeared under the water, the Hood and his team arrived at the Bank of England. The whole building shook as the Mole bored in from below. Once inside, they set about ripping open the safety deposit boxes …

Lady Penelope saw what was happening on Thunderbird 1's monitor. She jumped into a taxi and spoke to the driver. "The Bank of England, please."

• • •

Back at the monorail, Alan spoke to Fermat. "I'm going down in Thunderbird 4."

"F A B," said Fermat.

Alan steered the one-man rescue submarine to the sunken carriage and used a probe to cut through the bolts holding the car to the rail. "Shoot another line, Fermat!" said Alan, but Fermat hesitated. He was worried about hitting the passengers.

"I'll attach the line by hand," said Tintin. She dived into the river and

swam down to the carriage with a line. She attached it, then looked up, her breath nearly gone. The surface suddenly seemed a long, long way away.

Alan saw that she needed help. He steered the sub until it was close above her and opened the airlock. Tintin swam inside and was soon in the cockpit, taking great gulps of air.

Alan cut the last bolt holding the carriage to the rail and radioed Fermat. "These people need a lift!"

"F A B," said Fermat. "Commencing reverse thrust."

Thunderbird 2 rose slowly and the carriage broke the water's surface. Soon it was safely on the bank of the river.

"We did ..." said Alan, but his words were drowned out by rocket engines overhead.

Jeff Tracy and his other sons landed Thunderbird 3 just in time to witness the end of the rescue. But there was no time for celebration.

"Dad, Lady Penelope went after the Hood," said Alan.

"Then she may need our help," said Jeff.

"Can I offer you a lift?" asked a familiar voice.

"Parker!" said Alan. "How did you get here?"

"I came on one of Professor Hackenbacker's single-use shuttles," he replied.

"Good to have you here," said Jeff.

He and the team climbed aboard the shuttle and headed for the Bank of England. Alan was pleased to be with his father again, but there was a question he had to ask. "Dad, the Hood said you left him to die. Is that true?"

Jeff paused. "It's not that simple," he said. "The Hood kept his mine workers in chains. They couldn't run when the mine tunnels collapsed. We had to seal the mine, or hundreds more would have died. You can't save everyone. I had to make a choice."

Alan nodded. He understood.

●●●

In the vaults of the Bank of England, Lady Penelope had her gun trained on the Hood.

"Back into the corner," she told him but, before either of them could move, Mullion leapt forward and pinned her arms to her sides.

Lady Penelope sighed. "Now that's just not cricket."

Mullion snapped handcuffs onto her wrists and chained her to one of the cages filled with gold bars and jewels.

The Hood stood very still. He sensed that his enemies were near. "The Thunderbirds," he said. "They're here."

Mullion and Transom raced to meet them.

"Be sure to kill them," said the Hood. "All of them."

The Thunderbirds split up. Jeff and Alan took off to search for the Hood, leaving Parker and the others to take on Mullion and Transom.

When Tintin landed a kick on Transom, the Hood's ally took off after her. But Tintin was smarter than Transom, and soon the evil lady scientist was locked in an empty vault.

Meanwhile, Parker faced Mullion. "Try this," said Parker, landing a hard punch that made the goon stagger. Then a solid right-hand punch landed on his chin. This time Mullion hit the floor – and didn't get up.

Jeff was searching the main bank vault when the Hood stepped out of the shadows. He stretched out his hand, his eyes flashed black and Jeff shot into the air and landed in one of the cages! Before he could get to his feet, the door slammed shut and locked.

Alan was left to face the Hood alone.

The evil man walked slowly towards him, his black eyes glinting and gleaming. He waved his hand and Alan flew through the air, slamming into a wall.

Alan was winded and just managed to turn to one side as a piece of ceiling fell towards him. Then he got to his feet and charged at the Hood, who flipped into the air, soared up and landed on a metal catwalk far above.

The Hood moved his arm and Alan rose off the ground. It was as if some powerful, unseen hand had grabbed him.

The Hood sneered, and Alan fell to the floor.

But Alan could see that the Hood was losing some of his awesome powers. He was getting weaker.

The Hood went towards the Mole and Alan followed. But when Alan climbed the huge drill, its grinding teeth started to move! With one last effort, Alan launched himself into the air and grabbed for the catwalk. But he managed to grip it with only one hand.

"Goodbye," said the Hood, raising his foot ready to bring it down on Alan's hand.

Just then, Tintin raced in. She reached out her hands and waves of force and energy flew around the room. The catwalk tilted and Alan scrambled to his feet as the Hood toppled forward. Now HE was holding on to the metal bar with one hand!

Alan was safe, but the Hood was certain to fall to his death in the grinding teeth of the Mole – unless he was rescued.

Alan looked at the Hood long and hard as he dangled below him. He could see that, little by little, his grip was getting weaker.

But even now the Hood wasn't about to ask for help. "Leave me!" he spat. "Leave me to die!"

Then he relaxed his grip and his fingers started to slide from the metal bar.

Alan was still looking into his eyes when he reached forward and grabbed the Hood's wrist …

"I don't want to save your life," he said, still holding his gaze. "But I'm a Thunderbird – and that's what we do. Even for you."

• • •

The Hood was soon in the hands of the police. But he remained defiant. As he was led away he made one last menacing lunge at the Tracys. "See you soon," he said. "Very soon."

Minutes later, Alan, Jeff, Lady Penelope, Parker, Fermat and Tintin were standing beside Thunderbird 1, as Thunderbird 2 and Thunderbird 3 roared overhead and streaked off across the London sky, mission accomplished.

When they had disappeared into the clouds, Jeff turned to his youngest son. "I'm very proud," he said quietly. "You did a great job today."

Alan's face broke into a big grin. "Hey, does that mean I can drive home?"

Jeff smiled back. "No chance."

• • •

Safely back at the International Rescue base on Tracy Island, the whole team celebrated with a barbecue. The only member of the team who was missing was Parker. He was down on the beach, rebuilding FAB 1.

When Jeff clanged the big dinner bell, they all turned towards him.

"This is a special night," he said. "And we're all here thanks to three very special people."

He looked towards where Alan, Tintin and Fermat were standing.

"You three young people proved that the world needs the Thunderbirds – but the Thunderbirds need you, too."

He took three gold Thunderbird wing pins and pinned one on each of Alan, Fermat and Tintin's shirts. "You really earned these," he told them.

The teens looked down at the pins, then at each other, and grinned. For once, they were lost for words.

As the older Tracy brothers gathered round to congratulate them, Jeff's mobile phone rang. It was the red one, used only in times of emergency.

"Yes, Madame President," he said. "What's the problem?"

•••

Minutes later, the whole team raced into the control centre.

Brains, Lady Penelope, Fermat and Tintin stood at the International Rescue command console.

Jeff Tracy watched as, one by one, the older Tracy brothers took their places, standing below their pictures that were lined up along one wall.

First Virgil, then Scott, then John and finally Gordon.

But this time there was an extra picture hanging on the wall …

As his father looked on proudly, Alan walked forward and stood below HIS picture. It was quite a moment.

Jeff cleared his throat and spoke the words he'd said so often. As he started to speak, the picture wall flipped back and Alan and his brothers dropped down the chute that would take them to their Thunderbirds.

"THUNDERBIRDS ARE GO!"

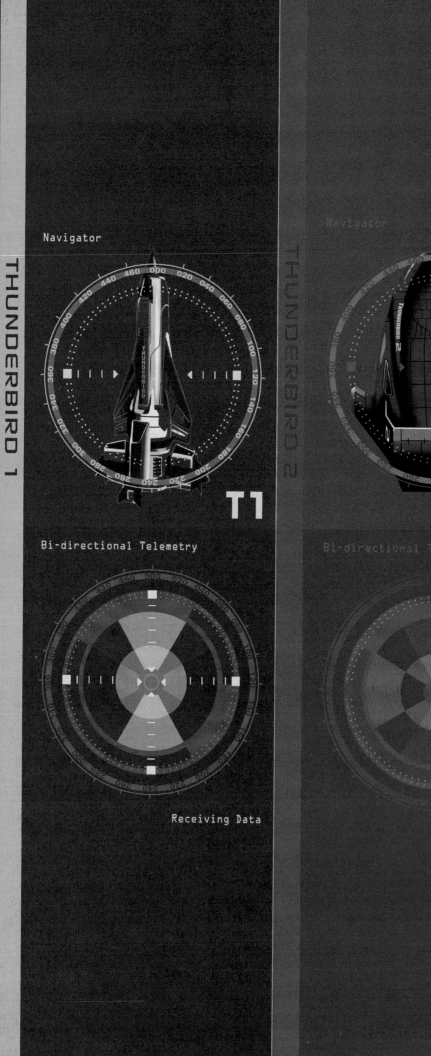

Navigator

THUNDERBIRD 1

T1

Bi-directional Telemetry

Receiving Data

Navigator

THUNDERBIRD 2

T2

Bi-directional Telemetry

Receiving Data

Navigator

THUNDERBIRD 3

Bi-direction